The School for Scandal

**An adaptation of the play
by Richard Brinsley Sheridan**

**Adapted by
Charles Jeffries
and Jerry Knight**

Baker's Plays
7611 Sunset Blvd.
Los Angeles, CA 90042
bakersplays.com

CHARACTERS

LADY SNEERWELL - In love with Charles and helping Joseph to connect with Maria.

SNAKE - Friend of Lady Sneerwell. Forger, disreputable.

JOSEPH SURFACE - A hypocrite, a backbiter, constantly delivering moral sentences and professing noble sentiments. Wants to have Maria at all costs. Has dallied, innocently…so far, with Lady Teazle.

MRS. CANDOUR - Mrs. Candour is a good-natured and friendly gossip who's talkative nature makes her dangerous, since she spreads slander more effectively than Backbite or Crabtree.

MARIA - Does not care for the ways of the world. Is an innocent ward of Sir Peter and Lady Teazle.

MR. CRABTREE - Crabtree is Backbite's uncle and as big a gossip as his nephew.

SIR BENJAMIN BACKBITE - Backbite is a suitor to Maria. He is a gossip who will slander anyone, even those he does not know. Lady Sneerwell admires Backbite's wit and poetry. Backbite is an especially malicious character whose rude behavior is encouraged in the company of his uncle, Lady Sneerwell, and Mrs. Candour.

SIR PETER TEAZLE - Maria's guardian, disapproves of Charles Surface, thinking he is attracted to his wife Lady Teazle. He has just married a younger woman who has come lately from the country and is caught up with town life.

ROWLEY - Friend and helper to Sir Oliver.

LADY TEAZLE - Has newly come from the country and married an older husband. She is quite caught up with the city and with these interesting people.

SIR OLIVER SURFACE - The uncle and benefactor of Charles and Joseph just returned to England from a long absence in the east. Wants to find out the truth about Joseph and Charles.

MOSES - Jewish money-lender.

CHARLES SURFACE (Joseph's Brother) - A prodigy and somewhat of a rake but he is frank, honest and generous.

SERVANTS TO LADY SNEERWELL

SERVANTS TO JOSEPH SURFACE

SETTING

The set has the look and feel of the historical, traditional lay out…a
door both left and right downstage at the proscenium arch. These
are the only two permanent items on the stage. As a scene in the
center is coming to an end, lighting is used to direct our attention to the area around either of these doors. At this time, servants
enter the darkened areas and set the necessary furniture items for
the next scene. Simplicity is the best idea, a settee, chair and small
table, which can be used for most scenes. Only specialized items,
bell pull, painting, mirror, screen, etc. will require special arrange-
ments…Essential items, no more.

ADAPTER'S COMMENTS

Sheridan's *The School for Scandal* is considered the finest example
of the 18th-century English Comedy of Manners. The playwright
captured the exact spirit, morals, language and character of the
age. How, then, to make it work for a modern audience without it
seeming like an archaic museum piece?

On closer examination, Sheridan has created characters and
themes of timeless humor and appeal. Although they may appear
fantastic, the characters must be treated as human beings in real
life situations. There needs to be a remembrance that this is a play
of verbal wit and dexterity.

The words are paramount. Slow and deliver the words…and we
mean the entire word. It is this humanity that we need to empa-
thize with and enjoy, as audiences have done for over 200 years.

–Charles Jeffries and Jerry Knight

To both of our families, the always wonderful, delightful and
helpful Lou-Ida Marsh, and to our students, over the years,
who understood and appreciated our favorite quote from
School for Scandal…

"There's no possibility of being witty without a little ill nature."

PROLOGUE

(spoken by one of the actors:)

Attend, ye virgin critics, shrewd and sage,
Attend, the living libel of a slanderous stage!
No need of lessons now,
We might as well be taught to eat…or plow.
With our friends we clashed - Alas!
The devil's sooner raised than stashed.
Our young Don Quixote - draws his pen,
And seeks his hydra, Scandal, in its den.
For your applause - he'll fight -
Till every drop of blood–think "ink"–is spilt for right.

SCENE ONE

(Minimal scenery is needed. It would be nice to have the traditional two doors downstage on either side of the stage for most entrances and exits in this production. This scene is a boudoir in Lady Sneerwell's house. There is a dressing table to stage right with a chair.)

*(***LADY SNEERWELL*** is seated looking into her mirror on the dressing table. At stage left there are two small chairs and a small table. ***SNAKE*** is seated on one of these small chairs, drinking chocolate and reading the "Society Items" Newspaper. His hat is on the small table.)*

*(***LADY SNEERWELL*** is attended by a ***HAIRDRESSER.*** He is just finishing up powdering her wig as the curtain rises. She surveys herself in the mirror and dismisses him with a wave of the hand. He bows and exits downstage right, closing the door behind him.)*

LADY SNEERWELL. The "special" paragraphs, you say, Mr. Snake were all inserted into the various papers?

SNAKE. *(lays down the newspaper and sips his chocolate)* They were, and best of all, *(He laughs.)* there will be no suspicion as to how they came to be there.

LADY SNEERWELL. *(checking the back of her hair with a hand mirror)* Oh, did you circulate the report of Lady Brittle and Captain Boastall?

(He rises and crosses over behind her at her dressing table and smiles.)

SNAKE. I did in that case, but in general, I am at a loss to guess your motives for these other actions.

LADY SNEERWELL. *(turning to him)* Will you never understand me, Mr. Snake? *(turns back to adjust her "beauty mark" on her face)* Long ago I was wounded myself by the tongue of slander. *(She lowers her voice.)* I know no pleasure equal to the reducing of others to the level of my own injured reputation.

*(***SNAKE*** assents with a nod.)*

SNAKE. But why should you be so earnest to destroy Charles and Maria?

LADY SNEERWELL. *(a little irritated that he has not figured it out)* Charles, the most handsome Charles, is one for whom I am thus both anxious and malicious – Maria – can be damned.

(She turns back and puts her dressing table in order.)

SNAKE. But then, why so confidential with Charles' brother, Joseph?

LADY SNEERWELL. Mr. Snake, you do require a lot of information. Joseph, like me, is selfish, and malicious, quite unlike his darling brother Charles...Maria is the one against whom we must direct our schemes.

(Enter a SERVANT.)

SERVANT. Mr. Joseph Surface.

LADY SNEERWELL. Well, show him up. He generally calls about this time. I don't wonder at people's believing him to be my lover.

(Exit SERVANT.)

(Enter JOSEPH SURFACE directly to LADY SNEERWELL with his stick and bouquet of forget-me-nots in his right hand and hat under his arm. SNAKE retreats up stage and is not immediately seen by JOSEPH.)

(LADY SNEERWELL extends her left hand. JOSEPH holding the tips of her fingers kisses her hand and at the same time presents the bouquet with his right hand over his left. She accepts it with her right and smiles in appreciation.)

JOSEPH. Lady Sneerwell...

(SNAKE comes down into the light. JOSEPH, seeing him says... in a very formal way)
Ah, Mr. Snake.

(They shake hands with the tips of their fingers, and then JOSEPH turns back to LADY SNEERWELL.)

LADY SNEERWELL. *(smelling the bouquet and laying it on the table.)* Tell me Joseph…when did you see your hoped for mistress, Maria – or what is more material to me, your brother Charles. *(She sits in her chair facing them.)*

(JOSEPH takes the closest chair, turns it to LADY SNEERWELL and sits.)

JOSEPH. I have not seen either but I can affirm that some of your stories have had a large effect on my hoped for mistress, Maria.

(LADY SNEERWELL Rises with happiness and crossing to SNAKE who is standing left of JOSEPH. She then turns back to Joseph.)

LADY SNEERWELL. Good, but do your brother's distresses increase?

JOSEPH. By the hour.

LADY SNEERWELL AND MR SNAKE. *(together, with a sigh)* Ah, poor Charles!

SNAKE. I believe, Lady Sneerwell, I'll go and copy the letter I mentioned to you…Mr. Surface. *(low bow)*

JOSEPH. Mr. Snake.

(SNAKE goes out of the door stage left but does not completely close it. He can be seen listening.)

I am very sorry you have put any further confidence in that fellow.

LADY SNEERWELL. *(Who has been fanning herself at left…stops.)* Why so? Do you think he would betray us?

(JOSEPH rises and crosses to the door and pushes it shut abruptly hitting SNAKE in the face. JOSEPH does not know that SNAKE was there.)

JOSEPH. Take my word for it.

(MARIA enters from stage right door.)

(JOSEPH upon seeing her is all chivalrous attention. Deep bow to her.)

Ah, Maria.

(LADY SNEERWELL crosses to MARIA right and touches fingers with her.)

LADY SNEERWELL. Maria, my dear…*(sits at her dressing table)* What's the matter?

MARIA. *(ignoring JOSEPH)* Sir Benjamin has just called, hoping to foster his odious uncle, Mr. Crabtree on me. So I slipped out.

LADY SNEERWELL. *(directing her to one of the chairs at stage left)* Is that all? Now, what exactly has Sir Benjamin done?

(MARIA sits in center chair.)

MARIA. Oh, he has done nothing; but 'tis for what he has said. His conversation is a perpetual libel on everyone he knows.

LADY SNEERWELL. Sir Benjamin is a wit and a poet. There's no possibility of being witty without a little ill nature.

(SERVANT enters left door.)

SERVANT. Madam, Mrs. Candour is below and, if your ladyship's at leisure, will leave her carriage.

LADY SNEERWELL. Beg her to walk in.

(Exit SERVANT leaving the left door open. She crosses to MARIA and takes her hand.)

Mrs. Candour is a little talkative, but everybody allows her to be the best sort of woman.

MARIA. She does more malice than most.

(Enter MRS. CANDOUR)

MRS. CANDOUR. *(as she curtseys)* My dear Lady Sneerwell, how have you been this century?

(Moves toward JOSEPH but midway she sees MARIA and goes on to her. JOSEPH bows toward her in frustration as she flies by. She reaches MARIA and bows.)

Ah, Maria, child! Is the affair off between you and Charles? His extravagance, I presume? The town talks of nothing else.

MARIA. 'Tis strangely impertinent for people to busy themselves so.

MRS. CANDOUR. People will talk.

JOSEPH. Oh, Mrs. Candour, if everybody had your good nature!

MRS. CANDOUR. I confess, Mr. Surface, I cannot bear to hear people attacked behind their backs. By the bye, I hope 'tis not true your brother is absolutely ruined?

JOSEPH. I am afraid his circumstances are very bad indeed, ma'am.

MRS. CANDOUR. So…let me make just a little note. *(She takes out a pencil and pad from her purse.)*

*(**SERVANT** enters door left.)*

SERVANT. Mr. Crabtree and his nephew Sir Benjamin.

(He exits)

*(**MARIA** starts to go out the other door but **LADY SNEERWELL** takes her hand and holds her in place.)*

LADY SNEERWELL. So Maria, you see how your lover pursues you?

*(Enter **CRABTREE** carrying a hat and stick. **SIR BENJAMIN** is heard talking offstage to someone.)*

*(**CRABTREE** takes **LADY SNEERWELL'S** hand and she curtseys.)*

CRABTREE. Lady Sneerwell.

*(Seeing **MRS. CANDOUR**, he moves to take her hand also.)*

Ah, Mrs. Candour, I don't believe you are acquainted with my nephew.

(He turns to introduce him and realizes he has not entered yet. Trying to fill time he giggles and says…)

He has a pretty wit – and a poet too, isn't he, Lady Sneerwell?

*(**SIR BENJAMIN** enters upon hearing his uncle going into a fluster.)*

SIR BENJAMIN. *(bowing to all)* Oh, Uncle!

CRABTREE. It's true. *(Seeing* **JOSEPH** *up stage left and crossing to him.)* Oh lord, Joseph, is it true that your uncle Sir Oliver is coming home from the East Indies?

JOSEPH. Not that I know of, indeed, sir.

CRABTREE. He has been in the East Indies a long time. You can scarcely remember him. I hear your brother Charles has gone wrong…

SURFACE. Charles has been imprudent.

SIR BENJAMIN. For my part I never believed him to be utterly void of principle as people say *(looking about and speaking in a whisper)* …though he has lost all his friends but the Jewish ones…

MARIA. Lady Sneerwell, I must wish you a good morning. I'm not very well.

(She exits upstage right off. It is quiet for a few seconds after her departure.)

MRS. CANDOUR. Poor dear girl.

(With a snort, **MRS. CANDOUR** *bounds off after* **MARIA.** *)*

LADY SNEERWELL. She could not bear to hear about Charles.

CRABTREE. *(confiding with* **SIR BENJAMIN**) Undone as ever a man was.

(Exit **CRABTREE** *and* **SIR BENJAMIN** *upstage right after* **MRS. CANDOUR,** *after a bow and a sniff.)*

*(***LADY SNEERWELL** *and* **JOSEPH** *moving down to the front of the stage on either side at the doors right and left then address the audience and each other. During this moment down front, servants enter and quickly change the set to the next scene, Sir Peter Teazle's house.)*

LADY SNEERWELL. Maria's affections are stronger than we imagined

(She turns to **JOSEPH** *across the stage.)*

JOSEPH. *(turning to her and the audience)* The family will be here this evening and we shall have the opportunity to observe her more closely.

(Bowing to each other they both laugh and exit thru the doors stage right and left and leave closing them together. A small snippet of music is played during the beginning of the change. The **SERVANTS** *continue to change the set as we see Scene Two downstage between the two doors left and right.)*

END OF SCENE ONE

SCENE TWO

(Sir Peter Teazle's house. The stage that will be set after this prologue between **SIR PETER** *and* **ROWLEY** *will consist of an armchair stage right, a settee center and a small chair to stage left. A bell pull is located stage right adjacent to the stage right door and a mirror is located on the left near the stage left door.)*

(This prologue scene takes place downstage between the Stage Door Right and Left. If possible the downstage should be the only lighted area during the prologue scene.)

(Enter **SIR PETER** *stage right…from outside. He carries a stick and gloves. He stops and hears* **LADY TEAZLE** *singing to a spinet accompaniment off left.* **SERVANTS** *rush in from the door stage right with many milliner's boxes and garment bags. They push by* **SIR PETER** *and exit to where* **LADY TEAZLE** *is through stage left door… into the house. The singing stops.)*

*(***SIR PETER** *moves to the audience and addresses them saying…)*

SIR PETER. When an old bachelor marries a young wife, what is he to expect.

(He turns away and then back to the audience…)

He deserves the punishment he gets.

(Enter **ROWLEY** *from stage door right. He is an older man who was at one time* **SIR PETER**'s *servant.)*

ROWLEY. Oh, Sir Peter, how is it with you, sir?

SIR PETER. Very bad, Master Rowley, very bad. Maria, my daughter…

ROWLEY. Nay, I'm sure she can't be the cause of your uneasiness.

SIR PETER. Why, has anybody told you she was dead? But the fault is entirely hers. In all our disputes she is always in the wrong. She refuses the man whom I have long resolved on for her husband, Joseph; – meaning, I suppose, she hopes to bestow herself on his profligate brother, Charles.

ROWLEY. You know, Sir Peter, Charles will correct his ways.

SIR PETER. You are wrong, Rowley. Joseph is indeed a model for all young men, but Charles…Ah, their father, Sir Oliver will be deeply mortified when he finds how part of his bounty is misapplied. Does he still wish us not to tell his nephews of his arrival?

ROWLEY. Most strictly.

SIR PETER. But pray does he know that I am married? And by the by, Rowley don't drop a word that Lady Teazle and I ever disagree.

ROWLEY. By no means.

> *(They exit together thru the stage door stage left.* **ROWLEY** *exits first…as* **SIR PETER** *is off a short ways we hear him complaining and he is pushed back on to the full stage from up left by* **LADY TEAZLE** *who enters pushing him. Full stage lights come up and we are in Sir Peter and Lady Teazle's home.)*

SIR PETER. Lady Teazle, I'll not bear it!

LADY TEAZLE. *(as she enters and comes to center laughing)* Sir Peter, you may bear it or not, as you please; *(curtsy)* but I ought to have my own way in everything—

SIR PETER. *(moves to armchair)* So a husband is to have no influence, no authority?

LADY TEAZLE. Authority? Well…no, to be sure. If you wanted authority over me, you should have adopted me and not married me. *(takes off cape and places it on chair stage left)* I am sure you were old enough.

SIR PETER. Aye – there it is. But you forget what your situation was when I married you. I have made you a woman of fashion, of fortune, of rank – in short, I have made you my wife.

LADY TEAZLE. *(admiring herself in the mirror at stage left.* Well, then—there is one thing more you can make me to add to that obligation, and that is—

SIR PETER. My widow, I suppose?

LADY TEAZLE. *(crosses to him and flicks him in the face with her fan)* Well, Sir Peter, if we have finished our daily jangle, I presume I may go to my engagements at Lady Sneerwell's.

SIR PETER. A Charming set of acquaintances you have made there!

LADY TEAZLE. Now, Sir Peter, they are all people of rank and fortune, and remarkably tenacious of reputation. *(Crosses to mirror to check herself. Gets her cape and begins to put it on as she crosses to the door at down right…)* Anyway, Sir Peter, you know you promised to come to Lady Sneerwell's too.

(Lighting is adjusted so that only the door at down stage right is illuminated. The scene change can begin at this point for the next scene.)

SIR PETER. *(stands at right and pulls the bell pull)* Well, well, I'll call in… just to look after my own character.

LADY TEAZLE. Then indeed, you must make haste after me, or you'll be too late.

(She offers her hand to him. He moves to her but decides to stop and bow. She takes it at that and departs. **SIR PETER** *crosses to the open door and throws a kiss after her. The door is the only lighted area at this point.)*

SIR PETER. Well though I can't make her love me, there is great satisfaction in quarrelling with her.

(He laughs to himself, briskly dons his hat and strolls out through the doors as the lights dim.)

END OF SCENE TWO

SCENE THREE

(In the darkness we hear a lady singing accompanied by a spinet. At Lady Sneerwell's House, in the drawing room. Lights come up on **LADY SNEERWELL** *as she enters from the door at downstage left and turns to talk off, to someone.* **SERVANTS** *have entered the acting space and are rearranging the set.)*

LADY SNEERWELL. No, positively, we will not hear it.

JOSEPH SURFACE. By all means.

(Lights come in generally and we see **SIR BENJAMIN**, **CRABTREE**, *and* **MRS. CANDOUR**.*)*

ALL. Yes, if you please.

SIR BENJAMIN. Tis mere nonsense.

CRABTREE. No, no, very clever.

SIR BENJAMIN. Well if you insist. I wrote these verses whilst on my ponies....

> "Sure never were seen two such beautiful ponies
> Other horses are clowns, but these *(pause for emphasis)*...macaronis,
> To give 'em this title I'm sure isn't wrong,
> Their legs are so slim and their tails are so long."

(He looks around for applause and approval. There is dead silence as everybody is trying to probe the sense of it. **CRABTREE** *and* **SIR BENJAMIN** *are crestfallen. Sir Benjamin repeats...)*

SIR BENJAMIN. ..."their legs are so slim and their tails are so long"...

CRABTREE. He did it in the smack of a whip and on horseback, too.

*(***SIR BENJAMIN** *seems much relieved and takes snuff and uses his handkerchief.)*

(Enter **LADY TEAZLE** *and* **MARIA**.*)*

(They cluster about **SIR BENJAMIN** *and he passes out copies.)*

MRS. CANDOUR. I must have a copy.

LADY SNEERWELL. Lady Teazle! I hope we shall see Sir Peter? *(looking at Maria)* Maria, my love, you look grave, come you should sit down with Mr. Surface.

(He swoops in to take her to be seated.)

*(**MRS. CANDOUR** has been chatting with **CRABTREE** and **SIR BENJAMIN**. She breaks away.)*

MRS. CANDOUR. You are so scandalous.

LADY TEAZLE. *(turning toward her)* What's the matter, Mrs. Candour?

MRS. CANDOUR. They'll not allow our friend Miss Vermilion is handsome.

LADY SNEERWELL. *(at center, commanding the space)* Oh, surely she is a pretty woman.

CRABTREE. I am very glad you think so, ma'am.

MRS. CANDOUR. She has a charming fresh colour.

LADY TEAZEL. Yes, when it is fresh put on. It goes off at night and comes again in the morning.

*(They all laugh except **MARIA** and **JOSEPH**.)*

MRS. CANDOUR. How can you be so ill-natured?

*(Enter **SIR PETER TEASEL**. All the ladies rise and he bows ceremoniously. The ladies curtsey to the ground and the gentlemen bow very low. **SIR PETER** has his hat under his left arm.)*

SIR PETER TEAZLE. Ladies.

MRS. CANDOUR. *(crossing to him)* Sir Peter. They have been so mean—and Lady Teazle as bad as anyone.

SIR PETER. It must be very distressing to you, Mrs. Candour.

MRS. CANDOUR. They will allow good qualities to nobody. Well, I never will join in ridiculing a friend—

CRABTREE. Oh, to be sure. She has herself the oddest countenance that ever was seen. It is a collection of features from all the different countries of the globe.

(laughter)

LADY SNEERWELL. *(seeing that Sir Peter is not amused)* Oh Lord, Sir Peter, would you deprive us of our privileges?

SIR PETER. Yes, madam; and then no person should be permitted to kill another's character.

LADY SNEERWELL. Go on, you monster! Come ladies, we shall sit down to cards in the next room.

(Enter a SERVANT who whispers to SIR PETER and exits.)

LADY SNEERWELL. Sir Peter, you are not leaving us?

SIR PETER. Your ladyship must excuse me; I'm called away by some particular business. *(He starts to exit and turns back to them)* But I leave my character behind me.

*(**SIR PETER** bows low and exits. They all exit grumbling and laughing into the next room.)*

JOSEPH. *(rising with **MARIA** and holding back)* I see you have no satisfaction in this society.

MARIA. How is it possible I should?

JOSEPH. *(crossing to her)* They have no malice of heart.

MARIA. *(raises her fan between them)* Then is their conduct even more contemptible.

JOSEPH. Undoubtedly. But can you, Maria, feel thus and be unkind to me alone?

MARIA. Why will you distress me by renewing the subject?

JOSEPH. Ah, Maria, but I see that Charles is still the favored rival for your hand. *(He fingers his sword hilt nervously.)*

MARIA. *(crosses him to the center as if to leave)* Be assured, I will not give him up.

JOSEPH. Maria—

*(He kneels. Enter **LADY TEAZLE** upstage…unseen by the two.)*

MARIA. *(turning and seeing **LADY TEAZLE**)* Lady Teazle!

LADY TEAZLE. *(to **MARIA**)* Child, you are wanted in the next room.

(MARIA sobs softly and exits. LADY TEAZLE follows her with her eyes, but does not move her head. MARIA turns and looks at JOSEPH. He throws her a kiss behind LADY TEAZLE's back. MARIA gives him a contemptuous look and exits. As LADY TEAZLE turns quickly to JOSEPH, he resumes brushing his breeches, down left.)

(He turns his back to LADY TEAZLE and says…in a halting manner.)

JOSEPH. I was just endeavoring to reason with her when you came in.

LADY TEAZEL. Indeed! Do you usually argue on your knees? *(Indicates the spot of the kneeling)* Come along, Joseph, we shall be missed.

(LADY TEAZLE exits the door right. JOSEPH moves to the door left as the SERVANTS enter to begin the scene change.)

JOSEPH. Now…but I am not sure how, I must become a more serious lover.

(He laughs it off and exits.)

END OF SCENE THREE

SCENE FOUR

*(The next scene is at Sir Peter Teazle's House in the
drawing room. It consists of a settee and small table
stage right and an armchair to the left of them. A bell
pull is located in the back.)*

(Enter **SIR OLIVER SURFACE** *and* **ROWLEY** *from stage
door right and down front.* **SERVANTS** *are setting the
stage behind them in the darkness.)*

SIR OLIVER. *(convulsed in laughter, with his stick in hand and
his hat on)* So my only friend is married, is he? Poor
Peter! *(He takes snuff.)* But you say he has entirely
given up on Charles—never sees him?

ROWLEY. His prejudice against him is astonishing.

SIR OLIVER. Well, I am not prejudiced against my nephew.
I promise you, if Charles has done anything false or
mean, I shall confront him.

(Lights come up generally and **SIR PETER** *enters from
up left.)*

SIR PETER. Well! Sir Oliver—my old friend. Welcome back
to England.

SIR OLIVER. Sir Peter! I am as glad to find you well. *(with a
look)* I find you are married, what?

*(**SIR PETER** gives him a look.)*

Well it can't be helped, so I wish you joy with all my
heart.

(Gives him a hug and they both move up stage with **SIR
OLIVER** *laughing heartily.* **SIR OLIVER** *stops and turns
to* **SIR PETER.***)*

And I am given to understand that one of my nephews
is a wild rogue?

*(**SIR PETER** refers **SIR OLIVER** to sit on the settee at right.
He does.)*

SIR PETER. Wild! Charles is a lost young man. *(turning back
to left and thinking it over)* However, the other of the
brothers, Joseph, is what a youth should be.

SIR OLIVER. Sir Peter, I don't mean to defend Charles' errors but before I form a judgment of either of them, I intend to make a trial of their hearts; and my friend Rowley, *(referring to him standing at stage right)* and I have planned something for that purpose.

SIR PETER. *(standing, crossing back and ringing for a servant)* What is the plan, Mr. Rowley?

ROWLEY. *(coming forward a little)* Well, sir, there is a certain Mr. Stanley related to them by their mother, he has been ruined by a series of undeserved misfortunes. He has sent letters to both, Joseph and Charles. From Joseph he has received nothing, while Charles is endeavoring to raise a sum of money, part of which, I know he intends for the service of poor Stanley.

SIR PETER. Well, yes, but how is Sir Oliver personally to—

ROWLEY. Why sir, I will inform Charles and his brother that Mr. Stanley has asked for permission to apply personally to them; and as neither of them has ever seen him, let Sir Oliver assume Stanley's person and he will have a fair opportunity of judging their dispositions.

(The **SERVANT** *enters with a tray with a bottle and three glasses and crosses to* **SIR PETER.***)*

*(***SIR PETER** *pours the wine and directs the* **SERVANT** *to give it to the men.)*

SIR PETER. Bah. Well, well, make the trial if you please. Do you have any other person who has examined Charles's affairs?

ROWLEY. Below, waiting our attention.

SIR PETER. Bring him in.

*(***ROWLEY** *makes a motion to the servant who exits out the right door with the tray.)*

ROWLEY. A, Mr. Moses.

SIR PETER. You suppose he will speak the truth?

ROWLEY. Oh, you may depend on his fidelity to his own interests. I also have another in my power, one Mr. Snake, whom I have caught in a matter of forgery. He knows I can have him jailed, so he will help us.

*(Enter **MOSES**. He bows a number of times and remains just inside the door.)*

SIR PETER. *(standing at settee stage left)* Honest, Israelite! This is Sir Oliver.

SIR OLIVER. *(rises and stands at his armchair stage left)* I understand you have lately had dealings with my nephew Charles.

MOSES. Yes, Sir Oliver. I did all I could for him but he was ruined before he came to me for assistance. This very evening I was to have brought him a person who will, I believe, advance him some money.

SIR PETER. Is this a person who Charles had never had money from before?

MOSES. A former broker.

SIR PETER. Sir, Oliver, a thought strikes me. Charles, you say does not know the broker?

MOSES. Not at all.

SIR PETER. Now then, Sir Oliver. Go with my friend Moses and become this broker.

SIR OLIVER. I like this idea better than the other, and I may visit with Joseph afterward as old Stanley.

*(Everyone seems to agree so **OLIVER** says to **MOSES**:)*

I'll accompany you immediately, Moses.

*(**SIR OLIVER** exits. **MOSES** bows and follows him out.)*

SIR PETER. So now I think, Sir Oliver will be convinced. You are partial, Rowley, and would have prepared Charles for the other plot.

ROWLEY. No, upon my word, Sir Peter.

SIR PETER. Well, go bring me this Mr. Snake, and I'll hear what he has to say.

*(Exit **ROWLEY**.)*

*(Enter **LADY TEAZLE**.)*

LADY TEAZLE. *(seeing him, she crosses to him and begins to fondle him)* Sir, Peter, I hope you haven't been quarrelling for I want you to be in a charming sweet temper at this moment.

(He smiles and moves toward her happily...)

Let me have two hundred pounds.

(All possible happiness is gone.)

SIR PETER. Two hundred pounds! What, can't I be in a good humor without paying for it?

LADY TEAZLE. *(starting to work her magic)* I assure you, Sir Peter, good nature becomes you. You look now as you did before we were married. I always said you'd make a very good sort of husband.

SIR PETER. And you prophesied right. And we shall now be the happiest couple –

(They both take hands.)

LADY TEAZLE. And never differ again?

(He takes her waist and directs her to the settee. They sit.)

SIR PETER. No, never.

(He touches her hair...she does not like it and pushes his hand away.)

Though at the same time indeed, my dear Lady Teazle,

(He pats her face...she doesn't like this either.)

you must watch your temper very narrowly, for in all our quarrels, my dear, if you recollect, my love, you always begin first.

LADY TEAZLE. I beg your pardon. Indeed you always gave the first provocation.

(He takes her arm, she unhooks him.)

LADY TEAZLE. While you to be sure–I say nothing ...but there's no bearing your temper.

(She rises.)

SIR PETER. No–no Madam 'tis evident you never cared a pin for me– I was a madman to marry you–

LADY TEAZLE. And I am sure I was a fool to marry you–an old dangling bachelor.

(She starts to walk away slowly toward the door stage right.)

*(***SIR PETER*** crosses to stage right as the lights go down to only this area. The scene change by the* ***SERVANTS*** *begins in the darkness.)*

SIR PETER. I have done with you, madam! I now believe the reports about you and Charles, madam.

(She turns on him. There is a pause.)

Yes, madam, you and Charles are…

LADY TEAZLE. Take care, Sir Peter. So goodbye.

(She turns, he thinks it over, but she just turns back to curtsey and then exits….laughing thru the stage door right.)

SIR PETER. *(crossing to the door and touching it)* Plagues and tortures. She may break my heart but she will not rouse my temper.

(He exits, losing his temper out the door right after ***LADY TEAZLE.*** *)*

END OF SCENE FOUR

SCENE FIVE

(The entryway of Mr. Charles Surface's house)

*(A **SERVANT** comes into the light and opens the door left. Enter **MOSES** and **SIR OLIVER SURFACE**. The servant bows and exits to tell **CHARLES** that he has company. The light is on them only as the other **SERVANTS** are changing the scene behind them.)*

*(It dawns on **SIR OLIVER** that he has forgotten his new name. He whispers to **MOSES**:)*

SIR OLIVER. Oh…Mr. Moses, what is my name?

MOSES. I believe you settled on …Mr. Premium.

SIR OLIVER. Yes, yes! *(looking at the door)* I believe this used to be my brother's house?

MOSES. Yes, sir. Mr. Charles bought if off Mr. Joseph with the furniture and even the pictures just as the old gentleman left it.

*(Enter **CHARLES SURFACE** as the lights come up generally. The room has an armchair at center with a table on either side and two smaller chairs left and right of the tables. In the background is a picture of **SIR OLIVER**. They all bow.)*

CHARLES. So, good to see you honest, Moses!

MOSES. Sir, this is Mr. Premium, a gentleman of the strictest honor and secrecy—Mr. Premium, it is…

CHARLES. Mr. Premium, the plain state of the matter is this: I am an extravagant young fellow who wants to borrow money. I know money isn't to be loaned without paying for it…

SIR OLIVER. Well – what security could you give?

CHARLES. Nothing…but I have a rich uncle in the East Indies, Sir Oliver Surface, from whom I have the greatest expectations.

SIR OLIVER. That you have a wealthy uncle I have heard… but, sir, as I understand you want a few hundred immediately. Is there nothing you can dispose of…nothing of the family property left?

CHARLES. Not much, indeed, unless you have a mind to the family pictures and if you have a taste for paintings…then you shall have them at a bargain.

SIR OLIVER. *(aside)* Oh, I'll never forgive him this! Never!

CHARLES. All yours… *(As he looks back at them, one strikes his eye.)* …but this picture here. *(He refers to Sir Oliver's portrait up stage.)* But, do let us deal, what do you say, Mr. Premium?

SIR OLIVER. Well, well, anything to accommodate you. They are mine: But what of this one portrait which you have passed over. *(He moves back to look at it.)* That ill looking great fellow.

CHARLES. Oh, that's my Uncle Oliver, painted before he went to India. That dear old fellow has been very good to me, and…I think I'll keep his picture.

SIR OLIVER. But sir, I have somehow taken a fancy to that picture.

CHARLES. I am sorry that you have, for you shall not have it.

SIR OLIVER. But sir, when I take a whim in my head, I don't value money. I'll give you as much for that as for all the rest.

CHARLES. Don't tease me. I tell you I'll not part with it and that's an end to it.

SIR OLIVER. Well, well, I have done. *(hands him some currency)* Here is the sum of eight hundred pounds.

CHARLES. What? *(more than he expected)* Eight hundred pounds!

SIR OLIVER. You will not let Sir Oliver go?

CHARLES. No!

SIR OLIVER. Then never mind the difference; we'll balance that another time. But give me your hand on the bargain. You are an honest fellow, Charles I beg pardon, sir for being so free. Good day. Come Moses.

(SIR OLIVER and MOSES move toward the left stage door. CHARLES moves back to the picture, looks at the picture and bows to them and exits. SIR OLIVER has stopped and sees this gesture. The lights fade down to only the area with MOSES and SIR OLIVER at the door stage left. SERVANTS enter to change the set for Scene Six.)

SIR OLIVER. ...But he wouldn't sell my picture...he would not sell my picture.

(Big smile. The door opens slightly and ROWLEY pokes his head in.)

Oh, here's Rowley.

(ROWLEY opens the door and stands in the doorway)

(greeting him) Sir. Well, well, I'll pay his debts...and now you shall introduce me to the elder brother Joseph as... Old Stanley.

(He goes out first followed by ROWLEY and MOSES thru left stage door.)

END OF SCENE FIVE

SCENE SIX

(Joseph Surfaces' House)

(The lighted area switches from the door stage left to the door stage right. Enter **JOSEPH SURFACE** *and* **LADY TEAZLE** *thru the stage door down right.* **JOSEPH** *enters first and holds the door for* **LADY TEAZLE**. *The* **SERVANTS** *continue to change the set in the darkness.)*

LADY TEAZLE. Have you been very impatient without me? I couldn't come till now. Upon my word, you ought to pity me. Don't you know Sir Peter has grown extremely jealous of Charles…And that Lady Sneerwell has circulated; I don't know how many scandalous tales of me and all without any foundation.

JOSEPH SURFACE. But, my dear. When a husband entertains a groundless suspicion of his wife, she owes it to the honor of her sex to outwit him.

LADY TEAZLE. Indeed! So the best way to curing him of his jealousy is to give him reason for it?

(The general light come up on the library in Joseph Surfaces' House. There is a large screen covered in maps of the world, stage left, which at this point is running from upstage to down and a settee stage right with a small table and a small chair.

(JOSEPH SURFACE enters the room. He takes one of the small chairs and brings it to **LADY TEAZLE** *to sit in. She remains standing, fanning herself)*

JOSEPH SURFACE. Undoubtedly!—what makes you impatient of Sir Peter's temper and outrageous at his suspicions? Why the consciousness of your innocence?

LADY TEAZLE. *(laughs as she seats herself)* Why, it is true. So–then I perceive that I must sin in my own defense–and part with my virtue to preserve my reputation.—

JOSEPH SURFACE. Exactly so.

LADY TEAZLE. *(taking his hands away)* Well, certainly this is the oddest doctrine.

JOSEPH SURFACE. *(moving a little from her)* An infallible one.

(A **SERVANT** *enters.)*

*(***JOSEPH SURFACE** *is very upset with him. He rises and crosses to strike the* **SERVANT**.*)*

JOSEPH SURFACE. What do you want?

SERVANT. *(shielding himself from any blows)* I beg your pardon, sir, Sir Peter is within.

JOSEPH SURFACE. Sir Peter!

LADY TEAZLE. Sir Peter! I'm ruined, I am ruined! What will become of me now, Mr. Logic? Oh, mercy, *(looks at the screen on stage)* I'll get behind here.

*(***JOHN** *sits down takes out a book that was on the arm chair to read as the* **SERVANT** *pretends to adjust his hair.)*

(Enter **SIR PETER TEAZLE** *from stage door right.)*

SIR PETER. Ah, ever improving himself!

(crosses to **JOSEPH SURFACE** *and pats him on the shoulder.)*

Mr. Surface, Mr. Surface—

JOSEPH SURFACE. Oh, my dear Sir Peter, I beg your pardon.
(He throws the book away and it bounces off the screen. He has a moment of fear that it will knock down the screen but it doesn't.)

I have been dozing over a stupid book. Well, you haven't been here since I fitted up this room.

*(***SIR PETER** *crosses to the thrown book and picks it up.)*

SIR PETER. It is very neat indeed. Well, well, that's proper; and you make even your screen a source of knowledge, all covered with maps.

JOSEPH SURFACE. On, yes, I find great use of that screen.

SIR PETER. I dare say you must. Certainly when you want to find anything in a hurry.

JOSEPH SURFACE. *(aside)* Or, indeed to hide anything in a hurry either.

SIR PETER. *(standing in front of the screen still)* Well, I have a little private business—

JOSEPH SURFACE. *(offering a chair at stage right)* Here is a chair, Sir Peter, I beg—

SIR PETER. *(walking about in front of the screen)* I wish to unburden my mind to you—in short, my dear friend, Lady Teazle's conduct of late has made me extremely unhappy.

JOSEPH SURFACE. Indeed!

SIR PETER. What's worse, I have it on pretty good authority to suppose she must have formed an attachment to another.

JOSEPH SURFACE. You astonish me!

SIR PETER. Yes; and, between ourselves, I think I've discovered the person.

*(There is a pause in which **JOSEPH** gives a sign and the screen moves a little.)*

…What say you to the possibility of your brother Charles Surface?

JOSEPH SURFACE. *(with great relief and humor)* Impossible! Besides…

SIR PETER. I wish to think well of her and to remove all grounds for quarrel between us. Here, my friend, are the drafts of two deeds, which I wish to have your opinion on.

(He takes out two bulky papers from his inner pocket.)

By one she will enjoy eight hundred pounds a year independent while I live, and by the other, the bulk of my fortune at my death.

*(He takes out a handkerchief and rubs his nose and eyes. **LADY TEAZLE** looks out and sees this action. **JOSEPH** signals her back behind the screen.)*

And now, my dear friend, if you please, we will talk over the situation of your affairs with Maria.

JOSEPH SURFACE. *(softly, looking toward the screen)* Oh no! Another time, if you please.

SIR PETER. Your passion for Maria is strong and I'm sure she's not your problem in the affair.

(Enter **SERVANT** *from stage door right.)*

JOSEPH SURFACE. *(happy to have a distraction from the subject)* Well?

SERVANT. Your brother Charles, sir is within.

JOSEPH SURFACE. Blockhead—when will you learn when I'm not within.

SIR PETER. Hold. A thought has struck me. Mr. Blockhead, tell him he is at home.

JOSEPH SURFACE. Well, then I guess I am at home.

*(***SERVANT*** exits.)*

SIR PETER. Let me conceal myself somewhere; then you tax him on the point we have been talking on. *(He moves to the screen.)* Here behind this screen will be– *(stops)* Well! What the devil! There seems to be one listener there already. I saw a petticoat!

JOSEPH SURFACE. *(laughs and quickly covering with a lie)* Well, that is ridiculous. *(taking his arm and trying to move him away from the screen)* I must admit it is a little French milliner that plagues me—and having some character, on you coming, Sir, she ran behind the screen.

SIR PETER. Ah, you rogue! But she has overheard all I was saying of my wife.

JOSEPH SURFACE. Oh, it will not go any further, you may depend on that. *(point off upstage right)* Well, please go in there.

SIR PETER. *(crosses to side and turns back)* Sly rogue!

*(***SIR PETER*** exits up off right.)*

LADY TEAZLE. *(peeping around the screen)* Could I not steal off now?

JOSEPH SURFACE. Keep close.

SIR JOSEPH. *(calling in from off right)* Joseph, press your bother for information about my wife.

JOSEPH SURFACE. *(to* **SIR JOSEPH** *off)* Back, my dear friend.

LADY TEAZEL. *(Peeping around the screen)* Couldn't you lock Sir Peter's door?

JOSEPH SURFACR. Be still my dear.

SIR PETER. *(voicing from off)* You're sure the little milliner won't blab?

JOSEPH SURFACE. In, in, my good Sir Peter.

(Crosses back toward the screen as **CHARLES SURFACE** *enters from the stage door right.)*

Lord, I wish I had a key.

(Enter **CHARLES SURFACE.** *)*

CHARLES SURFACE. Hello, brother. What has made Sir Peter steal off?

JOSEPH SURFACE. Hearing you were coming he did not choose to stay. To be plain with you brother, he thinks you are attempting to gain Lady Teazle's affections.

CHARLES SURFACE. Who? I? Or Lord, upon my word. That is funny.

JOSEPH SURFACE. This is no subject for jest, brother.

CHARLES SURFACE. I always understood you were her favorite. Don't you remember one day when I called here—

JOSEPH SURFACE. Charles—

CHARLES SURFACE. And I found you together—

JOSEPH SURFACE. Hush!

(He takes **CHARLES** *down front.)*

Sir Peter *(motions to door off)* has heard all we have been saying.

CHARLES SURFACE. How? Sir Peter? Where is he?

JOSEPH. There! *(points off right up)*

CHARLES. Lord, in front of heaven, I'll have him out here. *(calls off)* Sir Peter…come forth!

JOSEPH SURFACE. No, no—

CHARLES SURFACE. I say, Sir Peter, my old guardian, come into the room. *(He goes off up right and pulls him into the room.)*

SIR PETER. Give me your hand Charles, I believe I have suspected you wrongfully, but you must not be angry with Joseph. It was my plan.

CHARLES SURFACE. Indeed!

SIR PETER. I now know the truth.

JOSEPH SURFACE. Gentlemen, I beg your pardon. Could you meet me downstairs? I have a person coming on particular business.

CHARLES SURFACE. Well, meet him in another room I have something to say to Sir Peter.

JOSEPH SURFACE. *(as he exits he turns and speaking)* Sir Peter, not a word of the French milliner.

(He exits.)

SIR PETER. *(pulling* CHARLES *down front)* Well, have you a mind to have a good laugh at Joseph?

CHARLES SURFACE. I shall like it a lot.

SIR PETER. Joseph had a girl with him when I called.

CHARLES SURFACE. What! Joseph?

SIR PETER. Hush! A little French milliner. And the best part of the jest is—she is in the room now.

CHARLES SURFACE. The devil she is!

SIR PETER. Hush, I tell you it is true!

CHARLES. Ah, behind the screen? *(moves to it)* We'll have a peep.

SIR PETER. Not for the world.

CHARLES. I will cover for you.

SIR PETER. Careful here is Joseph.

(JOSEPH *enters just as* CHARLES *throws the screen to the floor.)*

CHARLES SURFACE. Lady Teazle—by all that's wonderful.

SIR PETER. Lady Teazle, by all that's damnable!

CHARLES. Sir Peter, this is one of the smartest French Milliners I ever saw. So I'll leave you to yourselves.

(Exit **CHARLES.** *They stand for some time looking at each other.)*

JOSEPH SURFACE. Sir Peter, I confess that appearances are against me—but I shall explain everything to your satisfaction.

SIR PETER. If you please, sir.

JOSEPH SURFACE. The facts, Sir that Lady Teazle, knowing my pretentious to your ward Maria—I say, sir—Lady Teazle, being apprehensive of your temper—she, sir I say—called her—I might explain these proceedings—but on your coming—being apprehensive—as I said—of your jealousy—she withdrew—and this, you may depend on it, is the whole truth of the matter.

LADY TEAZLE. I'll speak for myself.

JOSEPH SURFACE. The woman's mad!

LADY TEAZLE. No, sir she has recovered her senses, and your own arts have furnished the means. Sir Peter, I do not expect you to believe me, but the tenderness you expressed for me, when I am sure you couldn't think I was a witness to it, has penetrated so to my heart. As for that smooth-tongued hypocrite, while he affected honorable—I behold him now in a new light so truly despicable that I shall never again be able to respect myself for knowing him.

JOSEPH SURFACE. Sir Peter, Heaven knows—

SIR PETER. That you are a villain! And so I leave you to your conscience.

(He crosses to **LADY TEAZLE,** *offers his arm and the two exits thru the stage right door as* **JOSEPH** *runs behind blubbering.)*

*(***JOSEPH SURFACE** *is stopped at the edge of the stage by his* **SERVANT** *entering.)*

SERVANT. Mr. Stanley is below.

JOSEPH. Mr. Stanley. Oh, have you no sense at all! Do you suppose that I am now in a temper to receive visits from poor relations? *(pause)* Oh, well, show him up. *(**SERVANT** exits.)* I must try to recover myself and put a little…charity into my face.

*(**JOSEPH** crosses over to the stage door left to meet with **MR. STANLEY**. As he does so the lights go down and **SERVANTS** enter to change the set in the darkness. **SIR OLIVER** enters dressed as **MR. STANLEY** from the stage door left.)*

JOSEPH. Sir, Stanley is it? It is my understanding that you were nearly related to my mother. I presume you are in need of "assistance"? I wish I had it in my power to offer you some small relief, but I do not!

SIR OLIVER (AS MR. STANLEY). *(aside)* Dissembler! *(aloud)* Then, sir you can't assist me? Kind sir, your most obedient humble servant.

JOSEPH. Sir, yours as sincerely. *(turns and moves upstage into the darkness left)*

SIR OLIVER. *(aside as he exits thru the stage door left)* Charles shall be my heir!

*(Lights go out on the stage door left and come up on stage door right as **MRS. CANDOUR** and **SIR BENJAMIN** enters.)*

END OF SCENE SIX

SCENE SEVEN

(**SERVANTS** *in the darkness of upstage are changing the set to Sir Peter Teazle's house, which consists of a settee upstage on stage right. They also set up parts of the set for Scene Eight coming next which consists of the Library of Joseph Surface's House in Scene Six.* **SIR BENJAMIN** *enters first through the stage door right and turn back to* **MRS. CANDOUR** *who enters speaking.*)

MRS. CANDOUR. Oh, Sir Benjamin, you have heard, I suppose—

SIR BENJAMIN. Of Lady Teazle and Mr. Joseph Surface—

MRS. CANDOUR. And Sir Peter's discovery—

SIR BENJAMIN. Oh, the strangest business, to be sure!

LADY SNEERWELL. *(calling from off)* Mrs. Candour……

MRS. CANDOUR. (**MRS. CANDOUR** *hears a sound off stage thru the door.*) But here comes Lady Sneerwell; perhaps she knows the whole affair.

(*Enter* **LADY SNEERWELL** *pushing thru the door and past* **MRS. CANDOUR** *placing her between them as the lights come up to revel a hall way in Sir Peter Teazle's house. They are bunched up.*)

LADY SNEERWELL. So, my dear Mrs. Candour, have you heard the particulars?

MRS. CANDOUR. No but everybody says that Joseph Surface—

LADY SNEERWELL. No, no; indeed the secret meeting with Charles….

MRS. CANDOUR. With Charles?

LADY SNEERWELL. Yes, yes, he was the lover. Joseph was only the informer.

SIR BENJAMIN. I heard they began to fight with swords….

(**CRABTREE** *enters thru the open door and hears the end of the sentence. He pushes up against* **MRS. CANDOUR** *further crowding the group. Their heads swivel back and forth as each one talks.*)

CRABTREE. With pistols, nephew—pistols. I have it from an undoubted authority.

MRS. CANDOUR. Oh, Mr. Crabtree, then it is all true?

CRABTREE. Thought Charles would have avoided the matter if he could.

MRS. CANDOUR. I knew Charles was the person.

SIR BENJAMIN. Mr. Crabtree knows nothing of the matter.

CRABTREE. Do, nephew let me speak—

LADY SNEERWELL. *(aside, moving more to center.)* I am more interested in this affair than they imagine and must have better information.

(She exits by them all and out the door.)

*(Enter **SIR PETER** thru the stage door right. Seeing them he becomes very upset and moves toward them. He waves his stick.)*

SIR PETER. Fiends! Vipers! Oh, that your own venom would choke you!

*(They begin to run in circles to avoid him and then they exit **MRS. CANDOUR**, **SIR BENJAMIN** and **CRABTREE** quickly with great noise and fear out the stage door right. **ROWLEY** and **SIR OLIVER** happen to be entering and are caught up in this frantic exit.)*

ROWLEY. My, I could hear you outdoors and witnessed this departure. What has ruffled you, Sir Peter?

*(**SIR PETER** crosses back slightly on stage right and sits on the settee at center the lights come up full on the right side of the stage.)*

SIR OLIVER. *(crosses to **SIR PETER** and stands right of the settee)* Well, Sir Peter, I have seen both my nephews in the manner we proposed.

ROWLEY. *(by the door)* And Sir Oliver is convinced that your judgment was right, Sir Peter.

SIR OLIVER. Yes, I find that Joseph is indeed the worthy man, after all. He is a very model for young men of this age. Now, and how was your day Sir Peter?

SIR PETER. *(rises and crosses downstage center.)* Pshaw! Plague on you both! I see by your sneering that you have heard the whole affair.

ROWLEY. *(crossing a little to center)* Sir Peter, we are indeed acquainted with it all.

SIR OLIVER. *(crossing over to him)* Every circumstance.

SIR PETER. *(turning to them)* All?

SIR OLIVER. *(laughter begins to affect his speech)* Yes, even the little French milliner. Sir Peter, I should like to have seen your face when the screen was thrown down. *(big laugh)*

SIR PETER. *(can not hold it, even he seems the humor in it)* Yes, yes, my face when the screen was thrown down. *(Laughs…and then suddenly)* Oh, I must never show my head again.

SIR OLIVER. But it isn't fair to laugh at you neither, my old friend, though on my soul, I can't help it.

SIR PETER. Oh, pray don't restrain your mirth on my account. It does not hurt me at all. I laugh at the whole affair myself.

ROWLEY. Lady Teazle is in the next room. *(refers to upstage off right)* I am sure you desire reconciliation as earnestly as she does.

SIR OLIVER. *(begins to cross to the down stage door right)* Well, I'll leave Rowley to mediate between you. I am now returning to Joseph's if not to reclaim a libertine, at least to expose hypocrisy.

ROWLEY. We will follow.

    *(Exit **SIR OLIVER**.)*

ROWLEY. *(goes and looks off upstage right and says back to **SIR PETER**)* See, she is in tears.

SIR PETER. *(A little afraid to confront her…)* Don't you think it will do her good…to let her pine a little? *(**ROWLEY** signals, no.)* Well, I knew not what to think. You remember, Rowley, the letter I found of hers evidently intended for Charles?

ROWLEY. *(crosses back downstage by the stage door at right)* A mere forgery, Sir Peter, laid in your way on purpose.

SIR PETER. *(moving toward where she is off right, looking off at her)* What an elegant turn of head she has! Rowley, I will go to her.

*(**SIR PETER** exits to his wife and **ROWLEY** exits downstage door right.)*

END OF SCENE SEVEN

SCENE EIGHT

(The library in Joseph Surface's house. There is still the screen at stage left as it was before and a settee at center.)

*(Enter **JOSEPH SURFACE** and **LADY SNEERWELL** from upstage left into center.)*

LADY SNEERWELL. Impossible! *(crosses right)* Oh, I was a fool, an idiot, to league with a blunderer!

JOSEPH SURFACE. Sure Lady Sneerwell, I am the greater sufferer; yet you see I bear the accident with calmness.

LADY SNEERWELL. Because the disappointment doesn't reach your heart.

JOSEPH SURFACE. I don't think we're so totally defeated neither. Snake has undertaken to swear that Charles is at this time contracted by vows and honor to your lady-ship—which some of his former letters support.

LADY SNEERWELL. Indeed.

(A knock at the door.)

JOSEPH SURFACE. This is probably my uncle, Sir Oliver.

LADY SNEERWELL. I must hide.

(She crosses behind the screen at stage left.)

CHARLES. *(entering)* Joseph we must speak!

*(**SIR OLIVER** as **MR. STANLEY** comes rushing in from the downstage door at left.)*

JOSEPH SURFACE. Gad's life, Mr. Stanley, why have you come back to plague me just at this time? You must go away and stay away.

SIR OLIVER. Sir, I hear your Uncle Oliver is expected.

JOSEPH SURFACE. 'Tis impossible for you stay now, so I must beg—

*(Begins to push **SIR OLIVER** back to the downstage door left.)*

CHARLES SURFACE. What's the matter now? Don't hurt Premium.

JOSEPH SURFACE. *(moves back to center)* Mr. Stanley insists—

CHARLES SURFACE. Stanley? Why his name is Mr. Premium

JOSEPH SURFACE. No, no, Stanley.

CHARLES SURFACE. No, no, Premium.

JOSEPH. Well, no matter which. But—

CHARLES SURFACE. Oh, Stanley or Premium, 'tis the same thing as you say...

(knocking at the door stage right)

(JOSEPH SURFACE *moves to* **SIR OLIVER/MR. STANLEY/PREMIUM** *and begins to push him toward the door at left.* **CHARLES** *also comes to assist in getting* **SIR OLIVER** *out the door.)*

JOSEPH SURFACE. Here's Sir Oliver at the door. Now I beg you Mr. Stanley—

CHARLES SURFACE. *(with him)* And I beg, Mr. Premium—

SIR OLIVER. This is absurd.

(They both force him out the door but before they can suc- ceed, **SIR PETER, LADY TEAZLE, MARIA** *and* **ROWLEY** *enter from door at right.)*

SIR PETER. *(Entering first and seeing what is happening to* **SIR OLIVER.** *All call out his name...)* Sir Oliver—well! What in the name of wonder? Here are your dutiful neph- ews—assaulting their uncle on his first visit.

LADY TEAZLE. Indeed, Sir Oliver, it appears we have arrived in time to rescue you.

(After a pause, **JOSEPH** *and* **CHARLES** *turn to each other.)*

JOSEPH. Charles!

CHARLES. Joseph!

SIR OLIVER. Sir Peter, my friend, look at that elder nephew of mine and judge my disappointment in discovering him to be destitute of truth, charity and gratitude. As for that prodigal, his brother there—

CHARLES. To be sure, Sir Oliver, I did make a little free with the family canvas, but believe me, I feel at this moment the warmest satisfaction in seeing you.

SIR OLIVER. Charles, I believe you.

LADY TEAZLE. Yet I believe, Sir Oliver, here is one whom Charles is still more anxious to be reconciled to.

SIR OLVIER. Oh, I have heard of his attachment there; and with the young lady's pardon…

MARIA. Sir, I have little to say but that I shall rejoice to hear that he is happy. For me, what ever claim I had to his affection, I willingly resign.

CHARLES. Now, Maria!

MARIA. It is Lady Sneerwell. I know the cause.

CHARLES. Lady Sneerwell!

JOSEPH. Brother, Lady Sneerwell's injuries can no longer be concealed.

(He throws down the screen exposing **LADY SNEERWELL***)*

SIR PETER. So another French milliner! Egad, he has one in every room in the house.

LADY SNEERWELL. Ungrateful Charles!

CHARLES. Uncle is this another plot of yours?

JOSEPH. I believe there is sufficient evidence to make it extremely clear.

SIR PETER. Rowley!

ROWLEY. *(Crosses to door down left and opens it.)* Walk on in, Mr. Snake.

(Enter **SNAKE***)*

LADY SNEERWELL. Villain! Have you conspired against me?

SNAKE. You paid me extremely liberally for the lie in question, but I have been offered double to speak the truth.

LADY SNEERWELL. The torments of shame and disappointment on you all!

(She crosses to exit the door stage left, but is stopped by **LADY TEAZLE***'s voice…)*

LADY TEAZLE. Hold, Lady Sneerwell, before you go, let me thank you for the trouble you and that gentleman have taken in writing letters from me to Charles and answering them yourself.

LADY SNEERWELL. *(crosses to door left and stops)* May your husband live for fifty years.

(She exits)

LADY TEAZLE. What a malicious creature she is!

SIR OLIVER. Well sir, and what have you to say now?

JOSEPH SURFACE. Sir, I know not what to say. *(stammering for a moment)* I had certainly better follow her for her betterment.

(JOSEPH *exits quickly out the stage door down left.)*

(After he is gone **SIR OLIVER** *crosses to where Joseph has made his exit.)*

SIR OLIVER. Yes, and marry her, Joseph. Oil and vinegar… you will do well together.

ROWLEY. I believe we have no more occasion for Mr. Snake at present.

SNAKE. Before I go, sirs, consider. I live by the unpleasantness of my character and if it were ever given out that I had been betrayed into an honest action, I should lose every friend I have in the world.

SIR OLIVER. Well, well, we'll not say anything in your praise, never fear.

LADY TEAZLE. See, Sir Oliver. There needs no persuasion now to reconcile your nephew and Maria.

(They are standing apart holding hands.)

SIR OLIVER. Aye, aye…that's as it should be and we'll have the wedding tomorrow morning.

CHARLES. Thank you, dear Uncle.

SIR PETER. What, you rogue; don't you ask the girl's consent first?

CHARLES. Oh, I have done that a long time ago—above a minute ago—and she has looked a yes at me.

SIR OLIVER. May your love for each other never know abatement.

SIR PETER. And may you live as happily together as Lady Teazle and I… intend to do!

(All laugh and celebrate)

(General Bows)

END

www.ingramcontent.com/pod-product-compliance
Lightning Source LLC
Chambersburg PA
CBHW070421120726
47909CB00005B/1738